George Saves the World by Lunchtime

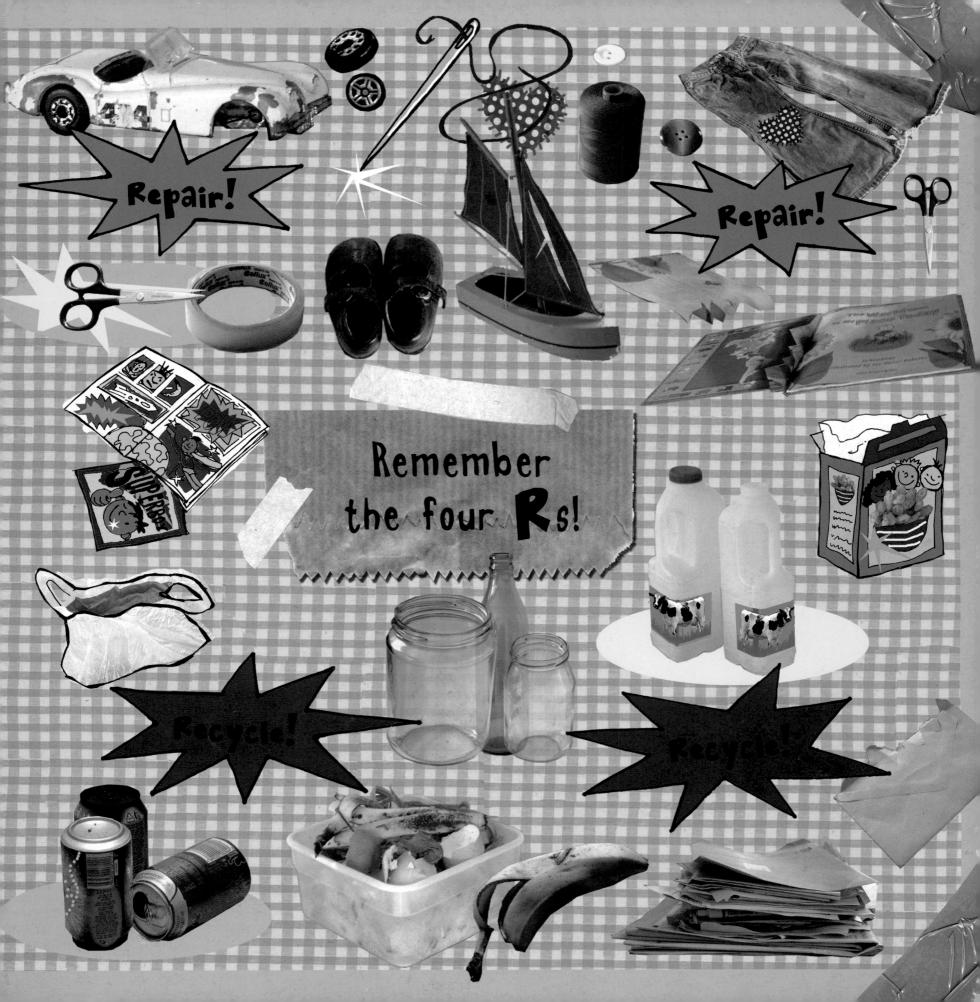

Repair!

Repair!

Remember the four **R**s!

Recycle!

Recycle!

*Thanks to all the children, young and old, who helped to
write this book by showing me how they are trying
to save the world by lunchtime . . . Keep it up! - JR*

For Ruby and her Grandpa Clive - LHR

GEORGE SAVES THE WORLD BY LUNCHTIME
AN EDEN PROJECT BOOK 978 1 903 91950 7

First published in Great Britain in 2006 by Eden Project Books,
an imprint of Random House Children's Publishers UK

13

Text copyright © Jo Readman, 2006
Illustrations copyright © Ley Honor Roberts, 2006

Photographs copyright © Eden Project, with thanks to Ley Honor Roberts, Bernie Hawes,
Dan Ryan and Glen Leishman. Glass and Newsprint photographs reproduced by
kind permission of Rockware Glass and Aylesford Newsprint respectively.

RANDOM HOUSE CHILDREN'S PUBLISHERS UK
61-63 Uxbridge Road, London W5 5SA
A division of The Random House Group Ltd

Addresses for companies within The Random House Group Limited can
be found at: www.randomhouse.co.uk/offices.htm

THE RANDOM HOUSE GROUP Limited Reg. No. 954009
www.edenproject.com

A CIP catalogue record for this book is available from the British Library.

Printed and bound in China

George Saves the World by Lunchtime

Jo Readman
Illustrated by Ley Honor Roberts

Eden Project Books

"What are you going to do today, George?"
asked Grandpa one sunny Saturday morning.
"Today," said George,
"I'm going to save the world!"
"Good plan!" said Grandpa.
"Flora and I will help you.
Let's see if we can save
the world by lunchtime."

George was keen to get on and save the world.
He quickly ate his breakfast and tossed his
leftovers in the bin.
"Slow down, George," said Grandpa.
"We might be able to use some of that again."

"But it's rubbish," said George, looking puzzled. "Aha," laughed Grandpa, "don't be too sure."

Tips for Saving the World by Lunchtime

Remember the four Rs.

Reduce!
Use less of everything.

Re-use!
Clean it up and use it again.

Repair!
Fix it and use it again.

Recycle!
Turn it into something else useful.

"Now, turn that light off, Superboy," said Grandpa,
"and then we'll hang out the washing."
"I don't have time to hang out washing," said George.
"I'm a world-saving superhero, you know!"

"EXACTLY," said Grandpa. "Saving
electricity will help you save the world."

Reduce!

Use less electricity.

Let the wind and sun dry the washing instead of a tumble dryer. Here's why:

Most electricity is made when giant magnets are spun round by jets of steam. The steam is made by burning coal.

Coal was formed millions of years ago when prehistoric forests rotted down into the earth. One day the coal will run low.

Burning coal causes pollution. People are trying to make cleaner electricity from the sun, the wind and the waves.

"Let's sort out your room now," said Grandpa.

"Let's not," grumbled George.

"I'm saving the world, remember?"

"We'll take your old stuff to a charity shop, then.
That will help save the world," said Grandpa.

"Humph," said George.

Re-use!

Even if you don't want your stuff any more, someone else . . .

can play with it again . . .

can read it again . . .

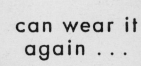

can wear it again . . .

Grandpa looked at George's broken car.
"I can fix that if you like," Grandpa told him.
"You'll have to do it this morning, Grandpa,"
said Flora, "if we're going to save the world
by lunchtime."

Charity shop

Repair!

Make things last longer by

sewing,

sticking,

taking them to the menders.

George and Flora went downstairs for a drink.
"We can sort the rubbish for recycling, now,"
said Grandpa.
"Oh, Grandpa, this isn't what I meant by
saving the world!" said George crossly.
"Maybe not," said Grandpa.
"But we're doing it for real."

plastic

cans

paper

glass

compost

"For real?" said George.
"Yes," said Grandpa, smiling,
"you've been saving the world all morning."

Recycle!

Two-thirds of all your rubbish could be recycled.

When you throw things away, you are also throwing away the materials, the time and the energy it took to make them. ⅓

Recycling saves those materials, time and energy. Rubbish in your bin doesn't just vanish. It has to be transported to a hole in the ground, called a "landfill site". ⅓

Much of it will stay there for ever. New landfill sites have to be dug all the time. ⅓

George followed Grandpa out into the garden.
"I was only playing a game before," he said,
"but I'd much rather save the world for real.
What can I do next?"

In the wild

Plants feed the animals.

Plants and animals feed the soil creatures.

Soil creatures feed the plants.

In Grandpa's garden

Plants feed the animals.

"Well, you can put **Floffy's** poo on the compost heap with all the other vegetable waste," said **Grandpa**.
"**Soon** it will turn into food for the plants."
"**Yuk**," said **George**. **He** was glad he wasn't a plant.
The **compost** didn't look at all tasty.

No glass, plastic or metal!
(Soil creatures can't make compost from them.)

Recycle:
In nature, plants feed animals and animals feed plants. No waste. No problem.

Plants feed the family.

George puts the waste on the compost heap.

Soil creatures turn the waste into compost.

Grandpa feeds the plants with the compost.

Plants feed the family.

"We'll go into town now," said Grandpa, "and do some recycling." "But we haven't got the car today," said George.

Reduce

Use less petrol. Walk, cycle, share with someone else, take the bus, the train or the tram.

Petrol is made from oil.

Oil was formed from millions of fossilized microscopic sea creatures.

One day oil will run low.

Burning petrol causes...

POLLUTION!

"So we'll cycle, which means we won't be wasting any –"

"Petrol?" said George.

"Exactly," said Grandpa.

One day we might use cars that are powered by the sun or the wind.

The charity shop in town was such fun that
George almost forgot he was saving the world.
"Say goodbye to your old clothes and books!"
said Grandpa.

"But say hello to a
fancy dress," said Flora.
Meanwhile George
had spotted something
VERY useful . . .

Re-use

When you take your old stuff to a charity shop, your clothes and toys can be re-used . . .

. . . and the money goes to help people who need it.

Next stop: the recycling centre. *Crash, tinkle, crunch!*
George was having a smashing time at the bottle bank.
"Now **none of** this will be wasted, will it?" asked Flora.

"No," said **G**randpa.
"It's all going to be turned into useful things again."

Recycle

This is what happens to the things you recycle:

glass

Glass is crushed and melted down to make more bottles and other glass objects.

cans

Aluminium drinks cans can be melted down and used again. This uses far less energy than mining new aluminium.

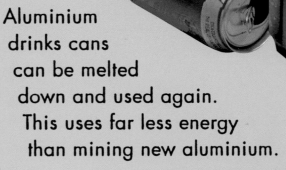
paper

Paper is pulped and made into more paper. It is also turned into bedding for your pets, or material to keep houses warm and save energy.

plastic

Some plastics can be recycled to make plastic bags, cups and plates and even fleecy tops.

Look out for things that are recyclable or made from recycled materials.

On the way home, Grandpa, George and Flora called in on the farmers' market.
"Can we take a break from saving the world now?" asked George. "I fancy one of those strawberry tarts."

"Don't worry," answered Grandpa, buying four of them. "Eating these strawberry tarts helps save the world, too. Oh, it's nearly lunchtime! We'd better cycle home!"

Reduce

...the distance things have to travel.

Things you buy at a farmers' market have been grown and made locally.

That means they haven't had to travel thousands of miles, using up petrol all along the way. They're fresh, so they're better for you.

MRS B'S STRAWBERRY TARTS — HOMEMADE WITH FRESH STRAWBERRIES, FREE-RANGE EGGS, LOCAL BUTTER AND FARMHOUSE FLOUR!

And then it was lunchtime!
"I hear you've been saving the world while I was out," said Mum.
"Yes," said George. "Grandpa helped us. He's a world-saving supergrandpa!"

"All in a morning's work,"
said Grandpa.
"I think I'll take a rest
this afternoon."